JUDY MOODY AND FRIENDS

Izzy Azumi, F.D.O.
(Future Dog Owner)

Megan McDonald

illustrated by Erwin Madrid

based on the characters
created by Peter H. Reynolds

CANDLEWICK

For Bobby
MM

To my daughter, Lena Kim Madrid
EM

Text copyright © 2023 by Megan McDonald
Illustrations copyright © 2023 by Peter H. Reynolds
Judy Moody font copyright © 2003 by Peter H. Reynolds

Judy Moody®. Judy Moody is a registered trademark of Candlewick Press, Inc.
Stink®. Stink is a registered trademark of Candlewick Press, Inc.

First edition 2023

Library of Congress Catalog Card Number 2022907292
ISBN 978-1-5362-2472-6 (hardcover)
ISBN 978-1-5362-2473-3 (paperback)

22 23 24 25 26 27 CCP 10 9 8 7 6 5 4 3 2 1

Printed in Shenzhen, Guangdong, China

This book was typeset in ITC Stone Informal.
The illustrations were created digitally.

Candlewick Press
99 Dover Street
Somerville, Massachusetts 02144

www.candlewick.com

CONTENTS

CHAPTER 1
Dogs on the Brain 1

CHAPTER 2
Fur Real 21

CHAPTER 3
Future Dog 41

CHAPTER 1
Dogs on the Brain

Dogs. Dogs. Dogs. Dogs. Dogs.

Fluffy dogs. Scruffy dogs. Curly-tailed dogs. Squirrely-tailed dogs. Pug-faced dogs. Ugh-faced dogs. Huggy dogs. Snuggly dogs. Dogs with spots. Dogs with dots.

From poodles to pugs, Izzy Azumi, F.D.O., loved them all.

"F.D.O. stands for *Future Dog Owner*," Izzy told her friends Judy Moody and Stink. "I'm going to have a dog of my own. Someday."

But someday never seemed to come.

Izzy asked her mom for a dog.
Again. "Please-pretty-please with
cupcakes on top?"

"This apartment's too small," said
her mom. "But I know your dad has
been thinking about getting a dog
someday."

There was that word again.
Someday.

Izzy gazed out the window of her dad's new house. The backyard even had an old doghouse in it. But no dog. A doghouse without a dog was like a birthday without a cake.

Izzy asked her dad for a dog. Again. "Please-pretty-please with pancakes on top?"

"We just moved in," said her dad. "We'll see."

We'll see did not mean *yes*. *We'll see* did not mean *no*. *We'll see* meant *maybe*.

Izzy told her older brother, Ian.

"Dad says maybe I can get a dog."

"Didn't he say *we'll see*?" asked Ian.

"Yes!"

"That means *no,*" said Ian.

Rats and double rats. Izzy Azumi was down in the dumps. "I don't know how much longer I can wait to get a dog," Izzy told Judy and Stink on their way to Wildlife Drawing Class. "What if I have to wait until I'm ten? Or *twelve*?"

"You're having fun pet-sitting Houdini," said Judy, trying to cheer her up.

"You still have Kiki," said Stink, hoping to make her feel better. "And don't forget Tankerbell."

It was true-not-false that Izzy Azumi already had some pets. She liked making fish faces with her goldfish, Tankerbell. She had fun reading aloud to Kiki, a South American pink-toe tarantula. And she loved taking their friend Rocky's spiny-tailed iguana, Houdini, for rides in the car with her dad.

"But have you ever tried to cuddle with a tarantula?" she asked her friends. "Or take a goldfish for a walk?"

Stink and Judy laughed their heads off.

A goldfish was not a dog. A
tarantula was not a dog. A spiny-
tailed iguana was not a dog.

A dog was furry. A dog was fuzzy.
A dog was fetch-y.

Best of all, a dog was a best friend.
A friend that loved you big. A friend
that loved you forever.

At Wildlife Drawing Class, Judy drew a snow leopard. Stink drew a megalodon. Izzy drew a dog. Not just one dog. Oodles of dogs. Poodle dogs. Dogs, dogs, dogs, dogs, dogs.

At Fur & Fangs pet shop, Judy looked for the hiding hedgehog. Stink petted the frog-eyed gecko. Izzy went straight to Mrs. Birdwistle's puppy. Mrs. Birdwistle owned the shop and often brought her puppy to work. Izzy let the pink-nosed puppy lick her whole entire face.

"Puppy licks are the best!"

After the Career Day fair, Judy told her friends she wanted to be a doctor.

"Just think. I can pass out Band-Aids all day."

Stink said he wanted to be an astronaut. "Just think. I can fly to Pluto!"

Izzy said she wanted to be a Professional Dog Walker. "Just think.

I can walk six dogs at once. Or seven.
Or eleven!"

"You have dogs on the brain," said
Judy.

"You have dogs on the brain," said
Stink.

"Woof!" said Izzy. All three friends
cracked up.

CHAPTER 2
Fur Real

On the way home from the fair with
Judy and Stink, Izzy looked for Missy
the dog walker, like she did every day.
As soon as she spotted the dogs, Izzy
Azumi, F.D.O., ran up to them.

"Hi, Fidget! Hi, Bridget!" she said,
petting a small wiener dog and a
large chocolate Lab.

A fuzzy dog jumped on Izzy. "Who's this cutie-pie?"

"Meet Ozzie. Ozzie is a mini Australian shepherd," said Missy. Ozzie had reddish-brown fur, white paws, and a white hourglass on her face. She had one brown eye and one blue eye.

"You're so cute. Yes, you are," Izzy said, rubbing noses with Ozzie. "Mini Aussies are my favorite dogs in the whole wide world."

"I thought cockapoos were your favorite," said Stink.

"Every dog is her favorite," Judy teased.

"But mini Aussies are my favorite of all favorites!" said Izzy.

"Ozzie is a cutie. And she had three puppies recently," said Missy.

"Puppies?" Izzy's eyes got big.

"Still a Future Dog Owner?" asked Missy. "No dog yet?"

Izzy sighed. "My dad says we'll see. But maybe if he met Ozzie's puppies, he'd say yes. I mean, who could say no to a face like this?"

"Sorry, Ozzie's puppies are already spoken for," said Missy. "But I know it'll happen for you someday. It's meant to be."

They waved goodbye to Missy. Ozzie gave each of them one last kiss.

"Dog kisses are slurpy," said Judy, wiping her face on her sleeve.

"Dog kisses are slimy," said Stink, wiping his face with his shirt.

"Dog kisses are the best!" said Izzy. She turned a cartwheel. Judy turned one, too.

They all flopped onto the grass in
Izzy's front yard.

"How come you want a dog so
bad?" Stink asked, pulling up grass.

"A dog is a best friend," said Izzy.

"You have *me*," said Judy.

"You have *me*," said Stink.

"I called best friend first," said Judy.

"So? I called it, too," said Stink.

"But I'm the one who asked Izzy to

teach me to do cartwheels," said Judy. "Now we cartwheel together."

"But I'm the one who found her tarantula when Kiki escaped," said Stink. "Now we tell spider jokes together."

"You're *both* my human best friends," said Izzy. "But I'd really like a furry best friend. A four-legged best friend. A *doggy* best friend."

"If you had a dog, what would you be doing with it right now?" Judy asked.

"Teaching it tricks," said Izzy.

"I bet we could teach your fish tricks," said Stink. "I had a goldfish once—Judy taught it to hula-hoop!"

"No lie," said Judy. "I got it to swim through a hoop."

"Let's try it with Tankerbell," said Izzy.

"We need a plastic ring and a chopstick," said Judy.

They ran inside. "Hi, kids!" Mr. Azumi called from the kitchen.

Izzy found a plastic ring from
around a milk bottle and a pair of
chopsticks.

"We're going to teach Izzy's fish
some dog tricks," said Judy.

Izzy's dad chuckled.

They went upstairs to Tankerbell's fishbowl.

"I'll hold the hoop in the water," said Judy. "You lead Tankerbell through the hoop with the chopstick."

Tankerbell swam to the left.

Tankerbell swam to the right.

Tankerbell swam up, up, up to the surface.

That goldfish swam everywhere *but* through the hoop.

"It's no use," said Izzy. "A goldfish is not a dog."

"I guess it's true," said Stink. "You can't teach an old fish new tricks."

"Maybe we can teach your tarantula a trick instead," said Judy.

Stink pulled a Ping-Pong ball from his backpack. "Let's teach Kiki to play fetch!"

"For real?" asked Judy.

"*Fur* real?" asked Izzy.

"Hardee-har-har," said Stink. He handed the ball to Izzy. "Toss the

ball across Kiki's tank. She just has to bring it back to you."

Kiki was hiding in her tunnel. Izzy showed Kiki the ball, then rolled the ball across the tank to the other end. "Fetch, Kiki. Fetch!"

"Fetch!" called Judy and Stink.

Kiki didn't budge. Not one bit. Not even a smidge.

"Wait!" said Stink. "She's coming out of the tunnel. Go, Kiki!"

Kiki trudged over to the ball and nudged it. The ball moved a pinch. The ball moved an inch.

"C'mon, Kiki. Bring the ball back to me."

"You can do it!" Judy cheered.

Kiki climbed over the ball. She climbed back. She pushed the ball again.

"She's doing it! Fetch, Kiki, fetch!" Izzy cried.

Kiki nudged the ball right up the side of the water dish. *PLOP!* The ball landed in the water. Kiki nudged the dish. The water dish turned over. *SPLAT!* Water spilled everywhere. Kiki hid inside her tunnel again.

"It's no use," said Izzy. "A spider is not a dog. If I had a dog, I could take it for a walk."

"Let's take Houdini for a walk," said Judy.

"We can walk him over to our house!" said Stink.

"Or up to Fur & Fangs," said Judy. "Or all the way to Screamin' Mimi's!"

"Yes, let's go!" said Izzy.

The kids ran downstairs. "Dad!" called Izzy. "We're taking Houdini for a walk."

Izzy put Houdini's special leash on him. She took him outside.

"Hi there, Houdini," said Ian. Houdini sniffed his shoe.

Houdini took a few steps. He climbed down Ian's skateboard. He stepped onto the sidewalk. He stopped.

"C'mon, Houdini," Izzy urged.
"Let's rock and roll."

Judy and Stink ran to the end of
the sidewalk. "C'mon Houdini." They
tried to coax him a little farther.

Every time Houdini took a step or
two, he stopped. He looked around.

The three friends did not walk Houdini to the Moodys' house. They did not walk Houdini to the pet shop. They did not walk Houdini to the ice-cream shop.

The three friends did not even make it past the mailbox.

"A spiny-tailed iguana is not a dog," Izzy said with a sigh.

"You need a dog," said Judy.

"For real," said Stink.

"Fur real," said Izzy.

CHAPTER 3
Future Dog

The next day when Judy and Stink
got to Izzy's house, she was writing at
her desk.

"Want to teach Houdini to roll
over?" asked Judy.

"Want to read *Time-Travel Tarantula*
to Kiki?" asked Stink.

"Sorry," said Izzy. "I'm busy."

"What are you doing?" Judy asked.

"Writing a letter."

"Who are you writing to?" Stink asked.

"I'm writing to my, um, pen pal."

Judy peeked over Izzy's shoulder.

Dear Future Dog,
My name is Izzy. You don't know me yet, but you will. I can't wait to meet you. Someday. We will kiss and cuddle. We will hula-hoop and play fetch and go for walks. I will be your forever family. And you will be my forever friend.
Love, Izzy Azumi, F.D.O.
P.S. Will someday ever come?

"Your pen pal's name is Future Dog?" asked Judy.

"Yes, I'm writing a letter to a dog. But not just any dog. A dog I'm hoping to get someday."

"Are you going to mail it at the doggy post office?" Stink asked.

"And will it get delivered to the doghouse?" Judy cracked herself up.

Izzy pointed out the window. "I'm going to put it in that old doghouse. It'll be kind of like making a wish."

"Rare!" said Judy. "C'mon, Stink. Time to go." They headed downstairs.

"Hey, kids," said Izzy's dad. "On your way out?"

Judy and Stink nodded.

"Before you go, I have some news." Mr. Azumi looked over his shoulder, glancing upstairs. He put his finger to his lips. He whispered to Judy and Stink.

Judy's eyes got big. Stink's eyes got bigger.

"What do you think?" asked Izzy's dad. "Want to help?"

"Sure!" said Judy.

"Let's do it!" said Stink.

Scribble, scribble, scribble. Judy and Stink got busy in a hurry. When they were done, they said goodbye to Izzy's dad.

"See you tomorrow?" he asked.

"See you tomorrow!" they said.

The next day, Stink felt like a Pop
Rock about to explode. Judy grinned
from ear to ear every time she saw Izzy.

On the way home from school,
Stink nudged Judy with his elbow.
Judy elbowed him back. Stink went
wink, wink. Judy went *wink, wink*
back.

"You guys sure are acting weird," said Izzy.

"Weird?" said Judy. "We're not acting weird. Are we, Stink?"

"Nope," said Stink. "We're not even acting strange."

When they got to Izzy's house, Izzy ran up the front walk.

"Izzy!" Judy called. "Don't you
want to get the mail?"

Izzy shrugged.

"You always get the mail," said
Stink. He opened the mailbox and
pulled out the mail. "Hey, look! You
got a letter!"

Izzy ran back to the mailbox. "I
wonder who it's from," said Izzy.

"Maybe it's from your pen pal," said Judy.

"Ha, ha, very funny," said Izzy.

"Open it, open it, open it," said Stink, bouncing on his toes.

Dear Izzy Azumi, F.D.O.,

I'm your pen pal. You don't know me yet. I can't wait to meet you. We will kiss and cuddle. We will hula-hoop and play fetch and go for walks. I will be your forever friend if you will be my forever family.

Love, Your New Puppy

Izzy's eyes got big. Izzy's eyes got round. "Dad!" she called, running into the house. "Dad! Look!"

Her dad and Ian were by the back door. Izzy waved the letter in the air.

"Guess what!" she said, out of breath. "I wrote a letter to my future dog, and *I got a letter back!*"

"How did *that* happen?" her dad asked.

Stink looked at Judy. Judy looked at Stink.

"Somebody must have read my letter," said Izzy. "I put the letter in the doghouse out back."

They all peered out the back door. "Let's go see if it's still there," said her dad.

Izzy flew outside. Everybody ran after her.

Izzy stuck her head inside the doghouse. The letter was not there.

But *something* was there. Something fuzzy. A jacket? A blanket?

A furry little bundle. A furry little bundle . . . of puppy!

Izzy couldn't believe her eyes.

"Surprise!" they all yelled.

A *puppy*? Could it be? Izzy squealed. The fuzzy puppy jumped right into Izzy's arms. It was puppy love at first sight. "She looks just like Ozzie!"

"Ozzie had puppies about two months ago," said Ian.

"But we had to wait until this little fur ball was old enough to adopt," said her dad. "I wanted it to be a surprise."

"And today is someday?" Izzy asked.

"Today is someday," said Izzy's dad.

Izzy hugged and cuddled and kissed her new puppy. She cooed, "You're so cute, yes you are," about a million times.

"What are you going to name her?" asked Judy.

"Pen Pal," said Izzy. "I'm going to name her Pen Pal."

Izzy rubbed noses with Pen Pal. "Hi, Pen Pal. I'm Izzy. Izzy Azumi, F.D.O. *Forever* Dog Owner."

Judy and Stink laughed.

Pen Pal tilted her head sideways at Izzy. She licked Izzy's ears. She licked Izzy's nose. She licked Izzy's whole entire face.

Izzy and Pen Pal. Pen Pal and Izzy.
It was meant to be.

Woof!